Dedicated to Rescue Dogs

RESCUE DOG

... and their handlers who sniff out drugs, bombs, and discover those who are lost or hurt.

res·cue dog

(noun) a specially
trained dog used
to find people who
are trapped,
cannot help
themselves,
or are dead.

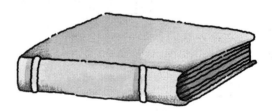

The Adventure Diary of... ™

Riley, the Rescue Dog!

By Carole Marsh

HEROES & HELPERS ™

Published by

GALL**O**PADE™
INTERNATIONAL

800-536-2GET
www.gallopade.com

Gallopade is proud to be a member of these educational
organizations and associations:

SHOPA *MEMBER*™
School, Home, & Office Products Association

NSSEA

HEROES HELPERS

The Adventure Diary of... ™

Other Great Heroes & Helpers Products!

Heroes & Helpers: Those Who Help Us Everyday and In Times of Crisis Book

Heroes & Helpers Activity Book

Heroes & Helpers Coloring Book

Heroes & Helpers Teacher's Thematic Book

Heroes & Helpers Careers Book

Heroes & Helpers Poster

Heroes & Helpers Sticker Fun Pack

Heroes & Helpers Card Game

Heroes & Helpers Bulletin Board Set

Table of Contents

Riley, the Rescue Dog!

Dedicated to Serve Others!

Day 1

Today my handler, Mack, was late with breakfast. I let him know it, too! I was barking loudly before he came. Mack is a specially trained dog handler, but he is also a police officer in the city's K-9 unit. Every morning, Mack brings my favorite dog food to fill up my bowl.

"Good morning, Riley," he greeted.

I gave him a friendly bark in response. After breakfast we played for a little while. I used to think that Mack was always losing things, the way he

Look It Up!

See page 42

<u>rewarded</u> me every time I found something for him. Now I realize that it is a kind of game. He hides a smelly towel or a sweaty piece of clothing, and after

I find it, I get to play with my favorite toy. I think I could chase that thing all day long!

"Good boy, Riley."

Day 2

Mack came and got me very early this morning.

"Let's go to work, Riley," he said.

I jumped into the truck and we

took off. We drove for awhile

before we got out. There were lots

of people standing around a

campsite. I knew there were a lot of

people there even before we

stopped. I have a nose for it.

Different people have different

smells; cologne, stinky feet, perfume,

hairspray, and last night's supper. I

smell other things, too: campfires;

pine trees; squirrels; coffee; and bug

spray. So many smells — so little time.

"Here boy," Mack called. "We'll find

your son ma'am," he said.

Mack was talking to another lady

who smelled like tissues and lotion.

She was crying. There were some

other people there, too. Mack let

me smell a teddy bear. It smelled like

a campfire, marshmallows, hot dogs,

bug spray, and oh yes – a little boy!

EMERGENCY!

"Do you smell that, Riley? Go get

it!" Mack shouted, and patted me on

the back. It's just like our game at

home. What am I going after? The

campfire? I ran quickly to the

campfire and stopped.

"No, Riley. Go get it." Mack held

the teddy bear again for me to smell.

I smelled the hot dogs,

marshmallows, and bug spray there,

too, but that's not what Mack

wanted. He wanted the boy!

Starting at the campfire, I circled

around stopping, wherever I got

the scent. He was there last night. I

wandered a little further until I

picked up the trail.

I found the little boy quite a

FAST FACTS!

Under certain conditions, some dogs such as bloodhounds are able to follow scent trails more than four days old!

ways into the deep woods. He was

curled up like a puppy, sleeping in tall

weeds. Mack patted my back and

rubbed my head when I found him.

"Atta boy, Riley!"

Day 3

Today, Mack took me to the school.

It was fun smelling all the little boys

and girls: chewing gum; pencils; old

books; and dusty classrooms.

There were so many kids, and they

all wanted to pet me – yeah! Mack

talked to them about dogs and the

different ways we help people.

"Some dogs are used

to find drugs. Some dogs are used

to sniff bombs," Mack explained.

"What do you use Riley for?"

asked a sweet-smelling little girl.

"Riley is a search and rescue dog,"

Mack went on. "Riley is trained to

find people who are lost or hurt."

A little boy who smelled like sloppy

joe and basketballs asked, "Has Riley

found a lot of people?"

"He hasn't lost anyone yet. Riley is

a real Hot Dog!" Mack said.

Day 4

Today, Mack and I went to the

training school for dogs. Sometimes

we go back to visit. I get to smell

some of my old trainers. There are

lots of puppies there just learning

the ropes. I remember what it was

like before I met Mack. It was fun,

playing hide-and-go-smell. It was a

good way for me to learn how to

find things, and what I'm looking for.

"There's Riley," greeted Linda,

one of my

Look It Up!

See page 42

old <u>trainers</u>.

"Woof!" I barked. I couldn't help

but wag my tail when I saw Linda.

She is so nice, and sometimes gives

me treats when I visit.

"That's a good boy." Linda

patted me on the head, and I licked

her hand as a greeting. I stuck my

nose in one of her pockets. I could

smell a dog biscuit in there.

"You know what I have, Riley," she

said. "Here you go, boy."

The school taught me how to find

people, but other dogs

learn how to find drugs, or

find explosives. There are all kinds

of dogs at the school: German

shepherds; Labradors; retrievers; a

few collies; and one time there was

even a poodle.

Linda and the other trainers

teach dogs not to be afraid of

earthquakes, fires, floods,

accidents, and many other types of

situations. We also learned

how to do the

Look It Up!

See page 42

doggie paddle.

She tests the dogs-in-training for

their sense of smell, strength,

endurance, good attitude,

intelligence, and loyalty. I passed

with a wagging tail. Hot diggety-

dog! Not every dog passes – it's a

dog eat dog world.

 # Day 5

"We're going to catch the bad

guys," Mack said. He was rushing

around very quickly. He opened the

gate to let me out, then stumbled on

a garden hose. I'm surprised he

doesn't fall flat on his face walking

around on only two legs. I checked

to make sure that he was OK.

"Dog-gone it. Let's go boy," he

said, as he hurried toward the

truck. We loaded up and took off.

Mack sped off to a wooded

swamp near the county jail. When

we got out I sniffed "Hello" to some

other dogs. There were

a couple of bloodhounds

and a Doberman pinscher with some

police officers. Another officer

passed a piece of cloth to Mack

and he let me smell it. I could smell a

man, cigarettes, concrete, and dirt.

"Riley, go get him," exclaimed Mack.

The other dogs and I took off like

we were in a race. We

Look It Up!

See page 42 searched in the

woods, the swamp, and all around a

creek, before we got the scent. We

followed his scent trail. It stopped

at a creek, but I knew that it would

pick up again on one side of the

creek or the other. All of us dogs

were sniffing. Mack and the other

officers kept encouraging us to

keep searching.

ALERT!

I was near the creek when I

caught a whiff of something. There

was a breeze blowing the scent

toward me. I followed the breeze

along the creek to a culvert, where I

pointed out the man hiding in a small

pool of water.

"You lucky dog," Mack said. I was

dog-tired.

Day 6

Something terrible happened

today. There was an earthquake.

Mack and I went downtown to

search for people in the rubble of a

collapsed building. There were many

people that escaped the building

and were unharmed, but there was

a lady trapped inside. I searched

for hours and hours. I did not want

to rest. I did not want to give up.

Finally I found the spot! Mack got

some people to help the lady out.

I was so glad when I found her,

but it sure was hard. My paws

were cut up on broken bits of

concrete and glass. Sometimes

after searching for a long time, I

get hot spots that are sort of like

bruises. Searching, digging, and

climbing in all that rubble is difficult

and dangerous — for me and Mack.

 **Day 7**

A man and two children came to

visit Mack and me today. The lady

we rescued was his wife, and these

were their children.

"We just wanted to thank you for

a job well done," the man said.

"Daddy, can we pet the dog?" the

children asked repeatedly.

When they came near, I thought

they smelled like their mother. They

patted me and hugged me and then,

they gave me a big T-bone steak!

"Riley is our hero!" they exclaimed.

"Woof!" I barked, thanking them

for the steak, and wagged my tail.

Riley the Rescue Dog Stuff!

RESCUE DOG

Dog House

Collar   Leash

Rescue

Sniff   Bone

Search

Trail

Dog toys

Scent

1. Was born to good parents. They had traits of good rescue dogs.

2. Trained hard in dog training school. Took a tour of a police station.

3. Trained hard with Mack, his new trainer. Went to the police academy.

4. Got his first job on the police force. Riley the Rescue Dog!

be A Rescue Dog!

5. Rescued his first person. Lived to tell about it.

6. Two years after Riley completed this diary of a week as a rescue dog he retired and now lives with his old partner Mack and his family.

Dog Tags!

Name: Riley

Occupation: Search and Rescue Dog

Likes: Doggy Bags

Dislikes: Dog and Pony Shows, Hot Dogs

Favorite Tree: Dogwood

Favorite Season: Dog Days of Summer

Favorite Sports: Dog Racing, Dog Sledding

Favorite Place to Sleep: Pup Tent
(No one likes being in the doghouse.)

Quote: "It's a dog eat dog world!"

That dog has personality!

Yes! Reminds me of myself.

A Rescue Dog's Poem

Riley!

There is a dog and his name is Riley,
He is the best search and rescue dog.
He can catch crooks no matter how wily,
Whether there's sun, rain, snow, sleet, or fog.

But there's something else he does
with great ease.
He finds people who are hurt or in trouble.
His handler Mack, Riley's eager to please.
"Get it Riley," Mack says "On the double."

Through woods, or swamps,
or dangerous fires,
Riley always finds the child, woman, or man.
Riley sniffs through wrecks, brambles,
or briars,
When no one else can find them, Riley can!

Look It Up!

You might know a little bit about what these words mean, but have you ever looked them up? Try finding out more about them in a dictionary, an encyclopedia, a CD-ROM, or another book.

- **reward**
- **dog trainer**
- **doggie paddle**
- **search**

Resources

Barry: The Bravest Saint Bernard
By Lynn Hall

Search and Rescue Dogs
By Charles & Linda George

Lighthouse Dog to the Rescue
By Emily Harris

Dog to the Rescue: Seventeen True
Tales of Dog Heroism
By Jeanette Sanderson

Mountain Dog Rescue
By Coleen Hubbard

Search-and-Rescue Dogs: Expert
Trackers and Trailers
By Elizabeth Ring

Post Card

RESCUE DOG

Tell a dog handler and rescue dog that you appreciate what they do!

Put Stamp Here

FROM:

TO:

Dear Dog Handler and Rescue Dog,

HEROES HELPERS

Riley's Doggy Dictionary

dogcatcher: someone who catches stray dogs

dog days: the hottest period of summer

dog-eared: having worn or well used pages

dog handler: a police officer or security guard who is in charge of a specially trained working dog

dog leg: a hole in golf in which the fairway has a bend

dognap: to steal a dog

dog tag: a metal identification tag for a member of the military, worn on a chain around the neck

dogwood: a tree or shrub that has clusters of small white flowers

About the Author

Carole Marsh is the creator of the Heroes & Helpers series. She is the author of *The Day That Was Different: September 11, 2001—When Terrorists Attacked America* and many other books.

Chad Beard is the Editorial Supervisor for the Heroes & Helpers series.

The character illustrations in this book were done by artist **Lucy Green**.

The book was designed by graphic artist **Cecil Anderson**.

Index

Dedicated to Serve Others!